# AN IMPATIENT GUY

## SAKSHAM SAXENA

*Dedicated to my parents.*

*Dedicated to my brother.*

*Dedicated to my friends.*

# Contents

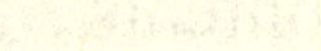

# ACKNOWLEDGEMENTS

Thank You!, dear readers, friends and my parents, for reading An Impatient Guy. Whatever I am today, are all because of your blessings. Thank you once again.

Manthan Saxena, My Brother, My first reader & editor.

All of your feedbacks till now are invaluable and also those which you will give after reading this.

Thanks to my father Mr. Manoj Kumar Saxena and my mother Mrs. Sapna Saxena who always motivated and supported me in everything.

Thanks to my family on YouTube, Facebook and Instagram.

**Saksham Saxena**

# PROLOGUE

This story is about Kush Bhatnagar. Kush Bhatnagar belongs from Lucknow, Uttar Pradesh. He is a very unstable guy and switches to many professions and streams in search of something. He keeps on changing his goals every day. He dreams many things but when the things come to achieving, he fails.

So, what is the reason behind his failures, his instability, you will get to know here through his story narrated in this novel.

The day begins with waking up from so many dreams in the mind and ends with the same lame questions How? And When?.

These dreams or let's say choosing a career started right away from the day when I just completed my High School from Lucknow. Dad asked, " Kush! , What's next!" , I replied, "Dad, I haven't decided yet."

Dad said, " In my opinion, you must head towards the commerce stream, as there are ample chances for you to build a stable career."

So, I started to think which branch to choose as, in my family we have Engineers, Architects, Managers, Administers, etc. I started dreaming, and started to imagine myself in each professions, that If I were this, what I be like! If I chose this.

So, I thought, " Why to take commerce, am made to be an engineer, and I should choose Mathematics and chose Mathematics as my dream field."

The day starts, I entered Mathematics, and I was unaware that there I'm going to meet a teacher that will leave such a great impact on me and change my whole perspective about Mathematics. Those were the days I really started to feel Mathematics not only as a subject but as my part of life.

After that, I somehow managed to clear my Higher Secondary studies. Mathematics was the only reason why I had to choose engineering for further studies and my Graduation.

As I have dreamt to be an Engineer. So, I entered in engineering immediately after that but before that there was again a big lame question aroused in front of me that which branch to choose, so I gave a thought and saw, as I liked electricity and magnetism so I chose Electrical and Electronics Engineering as my dream branch and entered into the engineering.

This was my first day of engineering, I was very excited since I started my college life in Lucknow and entered a new atmosphere. From the very first day, I interacted with so many new people, befriended some of them.

The real engineering started when I first entered in the workshop thing, I was really excited.

The Lab Assistant, Mr. Singh said, "Welcome Kush! How have you been? How you feeling as a 'to be engineer!' ".

I said, "Good Morning! Sir, It's amazing! I am really very excited for this and can't wait to get started."

So, that's the day I still remember the excitement I had on the very first day of my engineering. First year passed on so quickly, and now Welcome to the Second Year! As I must say that the real engineering starts. We consider second year as a foundation of your core branch.

The Head of Department, Mr. Rao from very first day was really impressed by me. As one can say, in his perspective I was a bright student, and all of my classmates I had a real passion for machines.

Mr. Rao said, "Welcome Class! From now on your real engineering starts". At that time, we felt thrilled after his class. That day we were delivered too much motivation and got filled with too much of enthusiasm.

Orientation day or we call it introduction session in front of our seniors or in other words ragging though it is banned. So, we can say that was the day when we were going to be groomed by our seniors about how to handle pressure, how to interact with our seniors etc.

Orientation starts, Firstly, We were asked to introduce ourselves on the podium and along with that we had to perform activities that were asked by our seniors to do one by one.

Many of my classmates were bit worried about the task.

I still remember about my friend Vishal that how worried he was that day. When he was called upon the podium to introduce himself, his legs was shaking because of hesitation and worry.

After that, I was being called by seniors on the podium to introduce myself, since I never had a stage fear thing this task was easy for me to perform. Tough part came when my senior, Mr. Navdeep, asked me to propose any senior with a red rose from his batch in front of everyone.

I thought it's just a cup of tea for me, I proudly went in search for Red Rose, and actually didn't found that anywhere in the college campus, except for one place, the garden behind Director's office.

Then, I found out why they have given me such a task. I haven't imagined that proposal will lead me to my suspension from college for a week. I still remember that incident it was such a memorable day.

After suspension, when I returned to college, my seniors said, "Kush! We are really impressed by you and thanks for saving us from the suspension. From now on we will support you and take care of everything.". From that day, my bonding with my seniors elevated to next level.

Slowly, I became the Class Representative or what we say CR because of my grades, communication skills. As, I interact almost with every senior and super senior of mine in every branch. From this, I got an opportunity to know about every branch from academics to placement scenarios.

This was the most memorable day of my life, when I was given the responsibility of Event Management in college, So, I was the Head of the Event Management committee of my college. I managed all things well, I also somehow managed to attract some cool sponsors for the event. As, I was good at academics so there is no doubt I was the branch topper since from the first year of engineering, at the end of every year event there is a prize distribution ceremony in which I every year wins the branch topper's trophy in my college. That day also I was called upon the stage to award me with that branch topper's trophy.

Since, I got too much idea about every branch, the time when final year came, I slowly begun to realise that the branch which I chose was not my dream branch.

As The Head of Department, Computer Science and Engineering, Mr. Agarwal, whom I will say sparked the light inside me. He said, "Kush! You are very much good at programming, and you must try for an IT sector MNC placement drive."

Hopefully, I appeared in the interview and also cleared and secured a job during pre placements of engineering.

Instead of everything else my interest shifted to IT sector because till that time ,during my final year pre placements period when I was offered a job by HCL Technologies, I realised that my passion is for coding and I must switch to software development for that. I rejected the offer from HCL Technologies

I have searched on Internet and found there are so many courses in ABC, So I filled up ABC entrance examination form and appeared for the examination and after that successfully cleared the ABC exam, and entered into ABC as I thought there I would get a higher package than College placements drives and would get a chance to explore and learn more about programming.

One day while exploring the courses of a ABC Noida, because after selection you have to give your choice about which subject you want to choose and study, I saw a course related to Remote Sensing and GIS.

After this I started dreaming about how would it be if I join ISRO or Defence. I immediately chose Remote Sensing and GIS and moved on with a new goal without forgetting about IT sector and development what we say sailing on two boats alongside each other and learnt both of them sincerely.

I was offered residential facility in ABC Noida campus, I immediately accepted that as because everyone must experience hostel life in his/her lifespan and as it is a saying that in hostel a person learns about the real life ethics and things.

I still remember the first day at the ABC Noida hostel, at some point I started to miss my home as everyone has home sickness at the starting.

Time passed by, I have made so many friends in the hostel.

Usually, we were having Saturday and Sunday as weekends, and as it was a Central Government funded Institute we had a off on both days. So, on Friday night we used to connect LAN in all rooms of the hostel and used to play Counter Strike whole night.

One friend of mine, Ketan, used to give a alarm call at each of our rooms, and that alarm call was 'Chalo Chalo' by knocking at each door and we all together proceed to mess for Breakfast and Dinner. Unlike every normal mess, Our mess used to have very delicious food.

I still remember, Birthday celebration ritual of my hostel, It was Yashwant's birthday, that day we have planned so much about that, and that stupid fellow undergrounded himself somewhere in hostel premises. That day while searching him we actually felt that we are part of any Intelligence organisation. We searched every room of hostel, every restrooms of the premises, we found him no where. One of my friend, from International students block posted a WhatsApp story, that see how Indian's celebrate there birthday, Accidentally, I opened that story and found that he was hiding inside Sean's room. We took a search party of 10 friends with us and carried him on four shoulders till our hostel. After bringing him to the corridor, we started to give him birthday bombs one by one , after that we bring him to his room and asked him to cut the cake and after that same thing decorated him with cake and all.

Time passed by, We created 'n' numbers of memories in the hostel. Now, it's the end of the session and also end of the residence, we started to vacate the hostel one by one. Helped each other in shifting and settling outside the campus.

Same condition arose here also after completion of the course, what's next? Because placements opportunity are almost nil in comparison to IT course placements which have a very good record. So I switched again to IT and landed in Capgemini in the pre placement drives with the knowledge of programming.

One day, I heard of a news that my friend Anil was selected and employed in Government sector.

I called him, "Hi Anil, How have you been?"

He replied, " Hi Kush! I am fantastic, want to give you a good news that I landed in my dream job and started my work in Government sector."

I wished him for his achievement.

After the placement drive, I came back to Lucknow to get set ready for Chennai as I was offered my posting at Chennai.

I started a normal conversation with my Dad and said, "Dad! You must be knowing Anil, he has started working in Government Sector."

Dad said, "Kush! I Suggest you must stay back and give one chance to yourself, for a Government Sector job."

I also started to think about this, days passed. On the day, when I was just few hours away to leave for Chennai immediately took a decision to stay right here and must try once for Government Sector job and switched my goal immediately.

Days passed, One day while surfing on the Internet, I found a University in Lucknow, is offering Masters degree in Renewable Energy Technology. I started to search its scope and placement opportunities in this field and after that I applied for the Master's programme in a University in Lucknow and my application was accepted by the university. The new phase of my life starts from here, with the new goal, Masters in Renewable Energy.

First day was quite good, everything was going well all classmates were good at nature and even the professors were also good. I got to learn many new things that day. While entering the Master's program I was unaware of the fact, that there I was going to meet such a professor who will leave a great impact on my thinking and knowledge. On starting, the master's degree program, I also gets fellowship from central government every month for my master's degree program since I was the branch topper and had decent grades in my Graduation course

I still remember the day, when we went on a solar site visit, actually it was not only a visit rather than it was a one day memorable trip to Nawabganj Bird Sanctuary. The responsibility for managing that trip was given to me by Prof. Mishra. I collected all the required contributions from everybody, and in the stipulated time made all the arrangements for the trip.

We started our trip at 08:00 AM sharp from the university campus, it takes almost 1:30 hrs to reach the site, during the trip journey all students enjoyed a lot in the bus. After reaching the site firstly we had done the case study on the solar plant setup present there. It took almost 2 hours to complete our case study. After completion of the study, our professors took us to visit the sanctuary. It was a memorable day.

One day, we were invited to Solar Summit Conference, there I got to learn many new things about the solar energy technology and even about the solar energy enterprises. After the conference, there were many solar energy technology business stalls, presenting each of their products to us, briefing each and everything about their technology. That was really knowledgeable day for me.

Days passed on, and the day comes when whole country or we can see whole world has just come to a stop. Yes, you guessed that right! CoVID-19 pandemic, hit the whole world including our country so badly that everything and everyone came to stop. Many of my near and dear one's lost their life amidst this pandemic. During those days, a tight locked down was imposed all over the country.

During the pandemic, I had done many constructive things as I had got enough time to think and brush up my skills. I had participated in Prime Minister's App development Challenge, yet failed. But, still managed to develop that app and test launched on Google Store and got certified as Google Certified Developer by Google. After that, I also developed a Website for university's particular departments and along with I also assisted my professor's in making department specific YouTube channel in order to help them in uploading their lectures online and creating live teaching sessions.

I also gave a thought amidst this pandemic, and planned to start something of my own and successfully started a YouTube channel of my own which was basically a Edtech channel. So, I started to upload video lectures of my own. Personally, telling it is way more harder to face the camera than to teach conventionally but after a lot practice now I became a pro. After watching my content, many friends of mine came forward and contributed there talents and knowledge in my venture and we became a team of 12 from a loan wolf and along with that we have together created a family of 500 subscribers in just 3 months. Slowly-slowly, everything started to come at a normal pace, also the imposed lockdown is also removed. Everything and everyone and every business started.

Now, there came the moment, the final year of master's, here also arises the same question, should I chose job or further studies. During this lockdown, I also got a chance to get to know a bit more about Prof. Mishra, she guided me through various things, cleared my every doubt and changed my whole perspective about my purpose of pursuing this master's degree programme, the thing which we call grooming, Prof. Mishra groomed me very well and made me understand the importance of studies.

Prof. Mishra called and said, "Kush! How have you been?"

I said, "I am very well Ma'am"

She further guided me and said, "Kush! In my opinion you should further study and must head towards research, because the research project which you have opted needs some final results and along with that this research project has very much potential and positive aspects and will contribute to the growth of Bioenergy in our country."

I gave it a thought, changed my goal of taking up a job and started to search the new goal and ways I can get admitted as a research fellow and found UGC NET as a pathway to enter into Research fellowship. So, I started preparing for UGC NET under the valuable and great guidance of Prof. Mishra. Though after so much failed attempts in UGC NET I once again changed my goal and focused on my EdTech channel which I have created in the pandemic.

By Now, every team member of mine left as they have some great opportunities after the pandemic. So, I was the loan wolf again. But, from here I never let my moral down. I started to teach multiple things and slowly-slowly started to get good analytics/responses on my videos. My family also supported me in all of these things, in the next 4 months being a loan wolf I managed to increase my YouTube channel family with 500 more subscribers and we have became a family of 1K+ subscribers.

The people who make fun of me and said, "What you have started, it's not worth as everyone is doing this plus you are bit funny in front of camera and you are just wasting your time, land yourself into a full time job, don't waste your parents money and efforts!", when I started this channel; slowly they started to become my supporters when I started to rise. These people including my friends, Teachers, Professors, Relatives all praises me of my efforts now.

The reason behind this Rise, is support of my family and friends. I had done some offline marketing like printing pamphlets and distributed to many nearby shops and asked them to stick pamphlets in front of their shops. I had applied some word to mouth techniques also. My friends also supported me a lot in this venture of mine by sharing my content attracting some customers to my channel, promoting my channel through their social media pages.

Now, everyone knows me by my Edtech channel, wherever I go. My teachers, say "Kush, The Founder of Edtech Channel". Whether, I visit any place or whether I attend any family function everyone signals me by "Kush, The founder of Edtech Channel". By Now, my Edtech is touching new heights everyday and with constant labour and efforts we are increasing our subscriber family day by day. Now, Along with some offline marketing techniques, I had been using some online techniques also which we call Digital Marketing.

Despite of changing so many goals in life, I finally came to a halt and sticked to my final goal that is of my Edtech channel.